DISNEY'S
My Very First Winnie the Pooh™

Safe at Home
With Pooh

Kathleen W. Zoehfeld   Illustrated by Robbin Cuddy

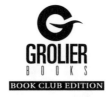
G
GROLIER
BOOKS
BOOK CLUB EDITION

Based on the Pooh stories by A. A. Milne
(copyright The Pooh Properties Trust).

Printed in the United States of America.

First published at Disney Press, New York, NY
This edition published by Grolier Books, ISBN: 0-7172-8867-6
Grolier Books is a division of Grolier Enterprises, Inc.

Disney's
My Very First Winnie the Pooh

Safe at Home With Pooh

One fine day Winnie the Pooh and Piglet were sitting together in their Thoughtful Spot, and when they happened to look up, Christopher Robin was walking down the path.

"Where are you going?" asked Pooh.

"To my grandma's house for supper," said Christopher Robin.

"You're going *out* of the Hundred-Acre Wood, b-by yourself?" asked Piglet.

"**M**y mom and dad say I'm big enough now," said Christopher Robin. "I know I can do it."

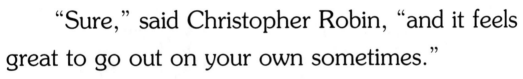

Piglet's ears twitched so hard he had to pull on them to make them stop. "Is-is it safe?"

"Sure," said Christopher Robin, "and it feels great to go out on your own sometimes."

"Not scary?" asked Piglet.

"It *was* a little at first," said Christopher Robin. "But my mom wrote down the Stay-Safe Rules for me. Once you know them, being on your own isn't scary at all."

"Can we learn the Stay-Safe Rules?" asked Pooh.

"Maybe *you* can, Pooh," said Piglet, "but it's too hard for a very small animal like me to stay safe."

"You are small," Christopher Robin said, "but you can learn to stay safe, too. The most important thing to remember is—don't ever talk to strangers."

"You mean people who look strange?" asked Pooh.

"Silly old bear," said Christopher Robin, "a stranger is someone you don't know."

"I do know Piglet," said Pooh. "And Piglet knows me."

"Right," said Christopher Robin, "and we all know Tigger, Owl, Rabbit, Gopher, Kanga, and Roo."

"And Eeyore," said Piglet.

"And Eeyore," added Christopher Robin quickly. "They are not strangers."

"Why can't we talk to people we don't know?" asked Piglet. "Are they d-dangerous?"

"Outside the Hundred-Acre Wood there are many, many people," said Christopher Robin.

"Hundreds?" asked Pooh.

"Thousands and thousands," said Christopher Robin. "Most strangers are nice. But a few aren't."

"How can we tell who's not nice?" asked Pooh.

"We can't tell the difference between a good stranger and a bad stranger just by looking," said Christopher Robin, "so we should never talk to any strangers."

"That doesn't sound very friendly," said Pooh.

"You can always be friendly with your friends," said Christopher Robin.

"It's nice to be friendly with friends," smiled Piglet.

"Yes," said Christopher Robin. "But you should never be friendly with strangers."

"Never . . . ," muttered Pooh thoughtfully.

"We can talk more later," said Christopher Robin, hurrying off. "I don't want to be late for supper!"

Well, the word "supper" reminded Pooh that he did not want to be late for *his* supper, either, so he invited Piglet over for honey and haycorns.

Pooh was just beginning his third pot of honey when Piglet looked up suddenly and listened.

"W-what was that?" asked Piglet.

"That's exactly what I was wondering," said Pooh.

"Oh, Pooh," said Piglet, "do you think it's a-a . . . a stranger?"

"It may be," said Pooh. "Sometimes it is, and sometimes it isn't."

*T*ap, *tap, tap*, went the noise.

"I think it's someone knocking at the door," said Piglet.

"Is that you, Tigger?" called Pooh. But it wasn't.

"Come in, Rabbit!" he said. But Rabbit didn't.

"What if it's just someone with a little pot of honey for us?" asked Pooh. He started to open the door.

"No!" cried Piglet. "What if it's someone we don't know? Remember what Christopher Robin said."

Piglet pushed a chair over to Pooh's window. He stood on tiptoe and peeked out.

"It's a very strange animal," cried Piglet, "with a shiny yellow head and big round eyes!"

Pooh looked, too.

Bang, bang, bang. The strange animal was hammering nails into a small board.

Pooh started to giggle. "He certainly looks strange, but he's not a stranger. That's Gopher. I forgot that I asked him to come over and fix my sign."

"It'ssss all fixsssed," whistled Gopher as Pooh opened the door.

"Thank you, Gopher," said Pooh. "Won't you come in for a cup of tea?"

"I could cccertainly ussse a sssip," said Gopher, pulling off his hard hat and goggles and wiping his brow.

Pooh had just set out the teapot when they heard another knocking. "Who is it?" called Pooh.

"It's me, Christopher Robin!" called Christopher Robin.

Pooh opened the door.

"Pooh, you really are a very clever bear," said Christopher Robin.

"I am?" asked Pooh. "What did I do?"

"You've learned another of the Stay-Safe Rules all by yourself," said Christopher Robin. "Always make sure you know the person at your door *before* you open it."

"I had a little help from my friend, Piglet," said Pooh. Piglet smiled proudly.

"Grandma gave me a bag of honey cookies to share with my friends," said Christopher Robin.

"Jussst in time for tea," said Gopher.

"Mmmm," said Piglet, "your grandma makes yummy cookies."

"The best in the whole world," said Christopher Robin.

"Can we have more, tomorrow?" munched Pooh.

"Now that you know the Stay-Safe Rules," said Christopher Robin, "you can come along to Grandma's house, and we can ask her together!"

CHRISTOPHER ROBIN'S STAY-SAFE RULES

- Don't talk to strangers.
- Never open your door to a stranger.
- Never take a present from a stranger.
- Never take a ride with a stranger.
- If a stranger does try to talk to you or touch you, yell "NO!" run away, and tell a grown-up you trust as soon as you can.
- And remember, if you're going somewhere, it's always friendlier and safer to go with someone you know.